WAYNEDALE

**DO NOT REMOVE
CARDS FROM POCKET**

Valentine Poems

Valentine Poems

SELECTED BY

Myra Cohn Livingston

ILLUSTRATED BY

Patience Brewster

Holiday House/New York

To David McCord

From: M.C.L.

Allen County Public Library
Ft. Wayne, Indiana

From: P.B.
x o x

MY HEART of HEARTS

To: Marietta Brewster Gregg

Library of Congress Cataloging-in-Publication Data

Livingston, Myra Cohn.
  Poems for Valentine's Day.

  SUMMARY: A collection of twenty poems which celebrate
Valentine's Day.
  1. Saint Valentine's Day—Juvenile poetry.
2. Children's poetry, American. [1. Valentine's Day—
Poetry. 2. Poetry—Collections] I. Brewster,
Patience, ill. II. Title.
PS3562.I945P6 1987   811'.54   85-31723
ISBN 0-8234-0587-7

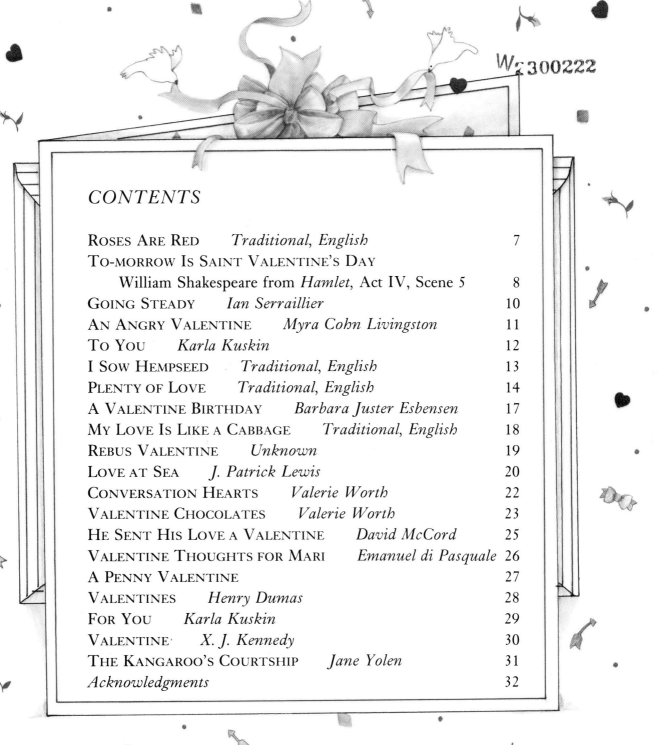

CONTENTS

ROSES ARE RED   *Traditional, English*   7

TO-MORROW IS SAINT VALENTINE'S DAY
   William Shakespeare from *Hamlet*, Act IV, Scene 5   8

GOING STEADY   *Ian Serraillier*   10

AN ANGRY VALENTINE   *Myra Cohn Livingston*   11

TO YOU   *Karla Kuskin*   12

I SOW HEMPSEED   *Traditional, English*   13

PLENTY OF LOVE   *Traditional, English*   14

A VALENTINE BIRTHDAY   *Barbara Juster Esbensen*   17

MY LOVE IS LIKE A CABBAGE   *Traditional, English*   18

REBUS VALENTINE   *Unknown*   19

LOVE AT SEA   *J. Patrick Lewis*   20

CONVERSATION HEARTS   *Valerie Worth*   22

VALENTINE CHOCOLATES   *Valerie Worth*   23

HE SENT HIS LOVE A VALENTINE   *David McCord*   25

VALENTINE THOUGHTS FOR MARI   *Emanuel di Pasquale*   26

A PENNY VALENTINE   27

VALENTINES   *Henry Dumas*   28

FOR YOU   *Karla Kuskin*   29

VALENTINE   *X. J. Kennedy*   30

THE KANGAROO'S COURTSHIP   *Jane Yolen*   31

Acknowledgments   32

ROSES ARE RED

Roses are red
Violets are blue
Carnations are sweet
And so are you.
And so are they
That send you this
And when we meet
We'll have a kiss.

Traditional, English

TO-MORROW IS SAINT VALENTINE'S DAY

To-morrow is Saint Valentine's day,
　　All in the morning betime,
And I a maid at your window
　　To be your Valentine.

WILLIAM SHAKESPEARE
from *Hamlet*, Act IV, Scene 5

GOING STEADY

Valentine, O Valentine,
I'll be your love and you'll be mine;
We'll care for each other, rain or fine,
And in ninety years we'll be ninety-nine.

IAN SERRAILLIER

AN ANGRY VALENTINE

If you won't be my Valentine
I'll *scream*, I'll *yell*, I'll *bite*!
I'll cry aloud, I'll start to whine
If you won't be my Valentine.
I'll frown and fret, I'll mope and pine,
And it will serve you right—
If you won't be my Valentine
I'll *scream*, I'll *yell*, I'll *bite*!

MYRA COHN LIVINGSTON

11

TO YOU

I think I could walk
through the simmering sand
if I held your hand.
I think I could swim
the skin shivering sea
if you would accompany me.
And run on ragged, windy heights,
climb rugged rocks
and walk on air.

I think I could do anything at all,
if you were there.

KARLA KUSKIN

12

I SOW HEMPSEED

I sow hempseed,
Hempseed I sow,
He that loves me best,
Come after me now.

Traditional, English

NOTE: *Repeated twelve times by a young woman circling a church in England to determine who would be her true valentine.*

PLENTY OF LOVE

Plenty of love,
  Tons of kisses,
Hope some day
  To be your Mrs.

Traditional, English

15

A VALENTINE BIRTHDAY
— *for Kai*

Again today
we draw the heart around
your name   Our red crayons
bright with love—
the paper white as drifts
outside the door

Snowfall on your birthday!
Each
tumbling flake snipped
into lace   by the   scissoring
wind
Valentines! Valentines!
Valentines!

BARBARA JUSTER ESBENSEN

17

MY LOVE IS LIKE A CABBAGE

My love is like a cabbage
  Divided into two,
The leaves I give to others
  but the heart I give to you.

Traditional, English

REBUS VALENTINE

You may not _____ all for me
    The way I care for you.
You may _____ your nose
    When I plead with you—
But if your _____ should _____ with mine
    Forever _____ hope
There is no reason in the world
    Why we two _____!

Unknown

Heart

Cantalope

Turnip

Lettuce

Beet

Carrot

LOVE AT SEA

February 14
Captain's Log
The Frisky Dog

Up through the fog came *The Frisky Dog*
  With me and my forty-man crew.
We were tightly packed, as a matter of fact,
  For *The Dog* is a bark canoe.
And the tides that ebb in the middle of Feb.
  Rolled in with a nasty howl,
But the crew stood fast to a two-foot mast——
  The flag was a paper towel.
Then the pop-eyed cook took a pop-eyed look,
  and he saw what we came to see:
The courtship swoon by a midnight moon
  Of an Octopus he and she.
They kissed on the lips and the slithery hips,
  They kissed on the suction cups.
And they bobbed in the brine like a ball of twine
  Till at last the bosun ups
And he shouts, "I'm Dutch, but I never saw such
  Sweet love on Valentine's Day!"
Then arm in arm . . . in arm . . . in arm . . . ,
  The Octopi swam away.

J. PATRICK LEWIS

20

CONVERSATION HEARTS

Such meek
Little tokens,
Sugary white,
Shy green, prim
Yellow and pink:

But spiced with
Mottoes: SURE
THING, OH BOY—
Each one like
A reckless wink.

VALERIE WORTH

VALENTINE CHOCOLATES

Ordinary candy,
Perhaps—but
Boxed in a ruby
Heart, it grows
Exotic, mysterious;
Not to mention
The red cellophane
Wrapper, which,
Looked through,
Shows a marvelous
Scarlet world.

VALERIE WORTH

23

HE SENT HIS LOVE A VALENTINE

He sent his love a Valentine;
His love did not reply.
We never *dare* to care to sign
These things, I wonder why.

David McCord

VALENTINE THOUGHTS FOR MARI

I'd like to bunch your lips
into a goldfish pout,
let fly your chestnut hair,
smooth the strands out of your eyes,
stroke your sparrow hand
and say, "Let's go where
the small brook frets.
Let's join
its silvery play."

EMANUEL DI PASQUALE

A PENNY VALENTINE

Silly, stupid, gawky elf,
Behold the portrait of yourself,
Dizzy, dozing, spiteful creature,
Mark each odious, hideous feature,
My heart shall never so incline
to choose *you* for a Valentine!

VALENTINES

Forgive me if I have not sent you
a valentine
but I thought you knew
that you already have my heart
Here take the space where my
heart goes
I give that to you too

HENRY DUMAS

FOR YOU

Here is a building
I have built for you.
The bricks are butter yellow.
Every window shines.
And at each an orange cat is curled,
lulled by the summer sun.
The door invites you in.
The mat is warm.
Inside there is a chair
so soft and blue
the pillows look like sky.
In all the world
no one but you
may sit in that cloud chair.
I'll sit near by.

KARLA KUSKIN

29

VALENTINE

If all the whole world's taxicabs
Came running to my call,
I'd park right by your door and honk
In the handsomest cab of all.

We'd drive to Spain, Maine, or Spokane!
Could anything be sweeter
Than ticking off a million miles
Upon a metal meter?

X. J. KENNEDY